sea MONKey Summer

A Richard Jackson Book

sea MONKey Summer

by CHeryl Ware

ORCHARD BOOKS
New York

J
WAR

Orchard Books, 95 Madison Avenue, New York, NY 10016

Manufactured in the United States of America.
Book design by Jean Krulis. The text of this book is set in 12 point
Usherwood Book.

10 9 8 7 6 5 4 3 2 1

Library of Congress Cataloging-in-Publication Data
Ware, Cheryl.
Sea monkey summer / by Cheryl Ware.
p.   cm.
"A Richard Jackson book"—Half t.p.
Summary: The summer before seventh grade, Venola Mae Cutright,
Belington, West Virginia's best newspaper carrier, writes a series
of humorous letters to her best friend away at camp, the Imperial
Magic Sea Monkey Company, and her newspaper boss.
ISBN 0-531-09518-5. — ISBN 0-531-08868-5 (lib. bdg.)
[1. Summer—Fiction. 2. Friendship—Fiction. 3. Newspaper
carriers—Fiction. 4. West Virginia—Fiction. 5. Letters—
Fiction.]   I. Title.
PZ7.W2176Se   1996   [Fic]—dc20   95-33523

For Mark, my family,
and circle of friends

River Road
Belington, WV 26250
May 2, 1996

Imperial Magic Sea Monkey Company
P.O. Box 2000
Destin, FL 32541

Dear Magic Sea Monkey People:

Please find enclosed six black specks. As you
can see, my Imperial kingdom of magic sea
monkeys kit did not grow like yours in the
magazine. Even with my brother Bobby's
magnifying glass, I cannot see their arms, legs,
tails, or their magic golden crowns!

Mama says I'm to request my money back—
including shipping and handling. However, if you
have a fresh batch of monkeys, I'm willing to try
again.

P.S. Please make sure the magic castle is
included. If they would of lived last time, them
monkeys might have been mad to have to live in

the same old Mason jar that I kept last year's lightning bugs in.

P.P.S. Yes, I washed out the jar and rinsed it real good before mixing up your magic monkey saline solution.

P.P.P.S. Please rush this order because I would like to be able to take them to show-and-tell before school lets out.

Sincerely,

Venola Mae Cutright

(My address is at the top of this letter because that's where Miss Montgomery, my sixth-grade English teacher, said it should go.)

River Road
Belington, WV 26250
May 15, 1996

Mr. John Casto
Circulation Director
The Elkins Exponent
Elkins, WV 26241

Dear Mr. Casto:

My name is Venola Mae Cutright, and I am
eleven years old. (But I turn twelve on October
12.) I am interested greatly in delivering papers
for your enterprise this summer.

My best girlfriend will be away at camp this July
and half of August, so I will have time to do a real
good job.

I come from a long line of paper carriers. My
brothers James, Melvin, Philip, and Bobby have all
delivered papers for you, and I'm sure you will
remember that they always worked real hard.
Katrina is my sister, but she has never delivered
papers for you because she is too uppity.

P.S. If you do not know of any routes available in my area, you will soon, because my brother Bobby wants to go to work as a bagger at Shop-N-Save grocery store as soon as he gets up the nerve to tell you.

P.P.S. I already know the route because I delivered them twice when he had diarrhea.

Sincerely,

Venola Mae Cutright

River Road
Belington, WV 26250
May 22, 1996

Mr. John Casto
Circulation Director
The Elkins Exponent
Elkins, WV 26241

Dear Mr. Casto:

 I don't know why everybody is mad at me. You'd think a family would be happy I've got the gumption to apply for a job.
 Bobby was getting ready to quit anyway, so what's the big deal who spilled the beans!?!?
 And he better stop calling me "Venola the Vulture," or I'll tell Mama and Daddy the next time he gets in trouble at school for not doing his homework or talking in class (which is at least once or twice a week).
 Please, please, please let me get that route!

Sincerely,

Venola Mae Cutright

P.S. Don't tell Bobby this letter is typed. He threatened to put Superglue on the keys the last time he caught me using his typewriter.

River Road
Belington, WV 26250
May 27, 1996

Mr. John Casto
Circulation Director
The Elkins Exponent
Elkins, WV 26241

Dear Mr. Casto:

   If it is okay with you, Mama says I can take over
Bobby's route under the following conditions:
   (1) I start a bank account and don't spend all
my money on junk food and stuff.
   (2) I promise to deliver them all by myself—
even when school starts back and even when it
snows.
   (3) My grades improve instead of drop. (Ugh!)
   (4) I quit nagging her about the route!!!
   Just to show you what a good salesperson I'll be
for you, I'll tell you how I convinced Mama to let
me have the route.
   At first Mama didn't want me to because "Only

boys deliver papers." Every time I brought up the subject, she said, "It's just not safe for girls—and anyway you're not old enough to be out alone."

The hair on my arms stood up straight when Mama said that "only boys" part. Over the past eleven years (almost twelve!), I've grown to hate those "only boys" words. You'd understand if you grew up with four brothers. "Only boys play football," Melvin or Bobby say when I ask to play with them and their friends. Or "only boys" go fishing or play gangsters or whatever else they are planning to do in the backyard that particular day.

Life ain't always easy with four older brothers!

Everybody tries to tell you that you are all equals, but if you're a girl, you can find yourself pushing a vacuum cleaner a lot more often than a lawnmower.

Oh, people always say "Why, Venola Mae, you're so lucky to have so many big brothers to take up for you when you've got problems," which makes my eyes bulge out and my eyebrows raise up about eight inches because they're usually the ones who cause my problems in the first place.

They hide my things, tattle when I take theirs, pull my hair, and throw stuff like pillows at me as I walk by, just to name a few. Bobby will go so far as to eat french fries right off my plate if I turn my head. (And it's starting to show on him, too. Oink.)

But when I tell on them, Mama says, "Boys will be boys," and she shakes her head and laughs at them when they give lame excuses like, "But, Mama, you call it a THROW pillow!" Unless she's plain worn out, and then she lets them have it. Her yelling at those gargoyles is the sweetest music my ears have ever heard.

But don't get me wrong, sometimes they can be nice. My brother James who runs the Union 76 station saves me Mallo Cup points so I can get free candy in the mail. Philip used to buy me chocolate milk shakes and carry me home from my dentist checkups when I was little, and now he lets me go to the drive-in movies with him and his girlfriend. And Melvin helped me with last year's science project. (I can't think of anything nice about Bobby right now, but that's probably just because he won't quit calling me "V-u-l-t-u-r-e.")

But back to how I convinced Mama to let me take the route. I'm sure you're a busy man with lots of papers to deliver yourself.

I had to put my common sense to work when Mama kept saying "NO" to the route. I said, "Mama, we know everyone in town from old man Teter to Mamie Holbert's youngest. Nothing is going to happen to me. I can't get away with nothing that you don't know about before I get home."

Mama kept peeling potatoes.

"Nobody said I was too young when Bobby had the trots and couldn't go last February, did they?"

She sighed, smiled, but kept peeling. I continued with my plan to wear her down, but I knew better than to push too far all at once.

I pretended to forget the subject and asked Mama what she had done after school when she was a girl. She relaxed and told about filling water jugs at a natural spring on the two-and-a-half-mile walk home, and about stopping to pick raspberries and being chased home by the yellowjackets that were protecting them.

I laughed at her stories, and then sneaked in a "How did it make you feel when your mama wouldn't allow you to do things just because you were a girl?"

Mama had grown up with SEVEN brothers. She put down the knife, dried off her hands, and laughed out loud. "Go deliver papers. You won't give me a minute's rest until you do, Venola Mae Cutright."

I disappeared down the hall to my room to write this letter before she had a chance to change her mind.

So let me know when I can start. Bobby has already showed me how to punch the ring of customer cards, and he says I can have his old canvas bag. As you probably know, he starts work at Shop-N-Save on June 7, the day that school is out. If you didn't already know, please don't tell Bobby I told you because I'm still in trouble for being the blabbermouth about him wanting to quit in the first place. Thanks.

Sincerely,

Venola Mae Cutright

(P.S. I promise to work really hard!)

River Road
Belington, WV 26250
June 1, 1996

Mr. John Casto
Circulation Director
The Elkins Exponent
Elkins, WV 26241

Dear Mr. Casto:

Yahoo! Thank you very much for this once-in-a-lifetime opportunity. I won't let you or The Elkins Exponent down—unless I happen to break a leg or something, and then one of my brothers—probably not Katrina—would help, so don't worry about anything.

I'll start tomorrow. Bobby is going to go with me to make sure I remember everything, even though I already told him he didn't have to.

P.S. Please send me some new hole punchers because Bobby's are not working right anymore. I would like to have some that punch hearts or clovers. If you are out or don't have such things, another pair like Bobby's old circle punchers will be fine.

Sincerely,

V. M. Cutright

River Road
Belington, WV 26250
June 3, 1996

Imperial Magic Sea Monkey Company
P.O. Box 2000
Destin, FL 32541

Dear Sea Monkey People:

Thank you for the new monkeys—and the additional bonus packet of Super-Stupendous Stalactites. (They look a lot like little colored sponges when they expand.)

Just one thing, I think they are really "stalagmites" unless there is something wrong with my packet. Tell your advertising people that my sixth-grade science teacher, Mr. Bookout, says to remember the "M" in stalagmite because the points point up whereas the "T" in stalactites point down. (Then he said, "If you can't remember that, just think "A stalagmite might reach the ceiling someday.)

Your people could probably reach him through

Belington Junior High if they have any more questions, because I do not have his home number because it is unlisted. (I checked the phone book for you.)

I think Mr. Bookout could help—just make sure he is in a serious mood. Sometimes he plays practical jokes like making us dissect earthworms on the day the cooks serve spaghetti and then making us dissect a fish on Friday (fishstick day!). I had him fourth period right before lunch, too! Yuck!

Well, anyway, he might be able to help you make sure your name is right.

P.S. If it isn't, maybe you could change the name of them to "Really Remarkable Radical Rocks." If I think of something better, I'll let you know.

Sincerely,

Venola Mae Cutright

June 16, 1996
Father's Day

Dear Daddy,

You are the best dad in all of Belington (and the rest of the world). I wanted to buy you the chain saw you've had your eye on at Wal-Mart, but I haven't sold enough papers yet. So, all I could afford was a spare chain for your old one.

P.S. If it's not the right chain, Bobby picked it out!

P.P.S. I.O.U. one deluxe chain saw next Father's Day.

Love,
Venola Mae

Monday

Sally Cathell
Pioneer Vacation Baptist Summer Camp
Dry Fork Road
Philippi, WV 26416

Dear Sally,

Sorry I can't be with you this summer at old
Pioneer, but now that I'm a working woman, I
can't be taking big long vacations all the time like
I did when I was in fifth grade and sixth grade.

How are things for you? Are you a Lady Coyote
again this year? Or did they move you in with the
Jackals? Who bunks with you????

Are you still the fastest swimmer? I bet you
are—unless you're too busy making googly eyes at
the boys. Any new ones? Too bad Sammy Potter
couldn't go. Then he wouldn't be pestering me
when I'm waiting for the papers in front of the
post office.

I wish you were here to walk around with me on the route. But I'll keep you informed.

Signing off,

VEN.

2 friends
+2 gether
———————
4 life

Thursday

Dear Sally,

Thanks for the update. I am glad you are a Jackal and that you-know-who smiled at you during sing-along. Maybe you were singing off-key. Ha! Ha!

Don't get mad at me! Of course you know you have THE best voice in sixth (I MEAN SEVENTH!) grade.

Things here are b-o-r-i-n-g!!!!!!!!!!!!!!!!!!! Want to trade places?

This whole paper route is more work than I counted on. A forty-pound newspaper pouch full of freshly printed papers that smell like paint thinner is awful hard on the neck and shoulders. Not to mention my ink-stained hands, face, and clothes. Mama says I look like Daddy when he comes home from the mines.

I can't ride my bike anymore because I keep tipping over to the right, especially on Wednesdays and Saturdays when all the businesses put in their sale flyers.

If you don't believe me, remind me to show you my scabby knees when you get home. Eight weeks and two days from today! That seems like forever.

P.S. You are missing some great movies on "Monsterpiece Theatre." So far since you left, our favorite vampire host Chilly Billy has shown <u>The Attack of the Killer Tomatoes</u>, <u>Killer Rabbits</u>, and our favorite, <u>Killer Spiders</u>. I watched Spiders this time without covering my head, except for once. Guess which scene?

Bye for now,

Venola

2 friends seperated
+2 long, seems like
———————————
4 ever

River Road
Belington, WV 26250
July 1, 1996

Mr. John Casto
Circulation Director
The Elkins Exponent
Elkins, WV 26241

Dear Mr. Casto:

Thank you for the nice white certificate with blue lettering. I hung it over my bed in a frame Daddy made. I couldn't decide whether to put it at the foot or the head, but I decided it would be better to look at when I first wake up.

Do you think I could get a new bag soon? Mine is dark dirty gray all the time even though Mama washes it with bleach twice a week.

P.S. Did you ever check your order book to see if that company made heart-shaped hole punchers? If not, that's okay. The diamond hole punchers you sent me are much prettier than

Bobby's pair that made big circles—except sometimes they get clogged if a customer pays more than three weeks at a time. (NOT OFTEN! HA. HA.)

Sincerely,

Venola Mae Cutright
Paper Carrier of the Month

Monday
July 1

Dear Sally,

Yes, I did forget that there is <u>a rat</u> in sep<u>arate</u>. Thanks for reminding me because Miss Montgomery would kill me. I can't believe I forgot that! Maybe I should practice this summer or she'll make me go back to "F" book with Sammy instead of moving on to "I" with you.

Too bad about you-know-who. Jerk! Missy isn't even that pretty.

Things here aren't any more exciting than your week. I pick up the roll of papers in front of the post office at 3:15 sharp, roll them up individually like Bobby showed me, and then snap a rubber band around each one. Then I stuff as many as I can in my bag. Now that I keep getting new customers (six this week!), I can't carry them all at once.

The rest, I have to come back for. I had been leaving them outside, but people must have thought they were free samples because the papers always disappeared by the time I returned. Then I had to BUY enough to finish my route.

Mrs. Gump has volunteered to store the extra papers behind the post office counter for me. But every day she says, "Uncle Sam could get me for this, Venola Mae, and if he totes me off to jail, I'm taking you with me."

She's kidding, don't you think? Why should he care if she stores a few papers for a half hour?

Sincerely,

V. M. C.

Paper Carrier of the Month!!!

P.S. If you add an "e" to your middle name, we would have the exact same number of letters in our names, and best friends really should according to this psychic on "Oprah." We will then be able to know when either one of us is in any kind of danger. I would drop my "e," but Venola Ma Cutright sounds A-W-F-U-L O-L-D!!!!!

Venola Mae Cutright   17 letters
Sally Ruth Cathell   16 letters

Ruthe or Cathelle—Which do you like better?

River Road
Belington, WV 26250
July 1, 1996

Imperial Magic Sea Monkey Company
P.O. Box 2000
Destin, FL 32541

Dear Monkey People's Bosses:

Enclosed is a Tupperware bowl of wet black specks. Please have your doctors analyze these in your laboratories. Please see if there is something wrong with <u>my</u> water. I follow your directions to a tee and even use Mama's measuring cup to mix up the saline solution, but don't tell her!!! Please help.

I await your quick response, and my NEW AND IMPROVED monkeys. Please hurry. It is only two months till show-and-tell starts again. Thank you.

P.S. I don't need any more magic rocks (sponges), but I never did receive the castle that is showed behind them monkeys in your advertisement.

P.P.S. Do you have to buy the little gold crowns sepearate?

Sincerely,

Venola Mae Cutright

Paper Carrier of the Month

Tuesday

Dear Sally,

Guess what?!? Mama let me open a checking account today down at One Valley Bank because she was tired of all the spare change laying around in my room. I think she was afraid we would (A) get robbed, or that (B) I'd spend it on junk. (Probably B!)

But she made me promise not to carry my checkbook to school this fall, which is no fun because what's the use of having one if I can't brag about it to Missy. Will you mention it to her for me?

I had a great time picking out my checks down at One Valley. I didn't know checks could be pretty and have artistic pictures on them, did you? Mama always uses plain olive green ones. Do your mama and daddy have pretty ones?

Birdie Johnson, the new accounts person, took my hundred-dollar deposit ($75 paper money and $25 Christmas/Easter/birthday money from Grandma). Then she reached me an order book as thick as a Webster's dictionary. I sat there looking at wildlife scenes, balloons, kittens, clouds, hearts, lightning bolts, Mickey Mouse, and at least ten different kinds of clowns.

I had just started through the book a third time when Birdie said the bank was closing in five minutes and that I would have to come back tomorrow, so I closed my eyes and pointed.

Now I'll be writing out my payments to the EXPO on Precious Moments checks. There are four different scenes. I'm never going to use any of the ones with three little girls jumping rope, because they are too cute to write on. Or I'll at least save them for special occasions.

I wrote my first check. I chose one of my least favorites with a little boy fishing, in case I messed up. I took my time writing out the "Pay to" column: "K-e-n-t-u-c-k-y F-r-i-e-d C-h-i-c-k-e-n" for "Twenty-seven dollars and $^{85}/_{100}$————————."

According to Birdie Johnson, you have to draw the line all the way to the end of the blank. If you don't, people can add extra numbers, and cause you to overdraw and bounce checks.

I can't wait until you get home. Only 46 more days. But I guess I shouldn't wish our summer away because the "s" word will be here before we know it—but at least we'll be in seventh grade!!

P.S. You wouldn't really throw the swimming

relay just so A.J. (oops, I mean you-know-who) could win, WOULD YOU?!?

P.P.S. I've picked up four more new customers. I'm up to 47!

Missing you,

Venola Mae
Paper Carrier of the Month

Wednesday

Dear Sally,

I didn't mean to brag about being paper carrier of the month, but it wasn't any nicer of you to point out that I was bragging than for me to do it. Sorry. Don't be mad.

Sincerely,

V.

$$\begin{array}{r} 2 \text{ good of friends} \\ +\ 2 \text{ stay mad} \\ \hline 4 \text{ very long} \end{array}$$

Thursday, late
July 4

Dear Sally,

Did the camp have fireworks this year? We went to the fairgrounds and had a family picnic.

It was kind of boring without you there to talk to me.

Your friend,
Venola Mae

2 friends
+2 far apart on
4th of July

Friday

Dear Sally,

No, I didn't eat $27 worth of chicken by myself!!! Did I not tell you I took my family out to eat? Bobby ate four pieces—three white and one leg.

Yes, I had forgotten your mama had those checks with the flowers on them down at her floral shop. But mine with the Precious Moments figures are lots prettier—like cartoons. I can't wait for you to see them.

Latest packet of monkeys arrived. Maybe there is something wrong with their packaging techniques. Because they are just like specks of dried pepper when I receive them in a packet no bigger than Mama's bread yeast. This time after three days, they turned white and started squirming around, but then the little white specks dried up and stuck to the side of the jar. Why can't they send them UPS in a tank with the castle already set up? I'd pay the difference.

Congratulations on attracting A.J. I feel as bad as

you about Missy's unfortunate bout of hives or whatever cooties she has caught. Are you sure it's all right to put his name in? What about spies?!? You didn't cause them hives did you?

Got to go. Mama's yelling for me to set the table for supper. BYE!

Venola Mae

Saturday
July 6

Dear Sally,

   My life is over. Remember those two warts I had
on the bottom of my left foot? They are
spreading!!!

   Please don't tell Missy. I have tried all them
over-the-counter medicines, including Compound
W, but they haven't done anything but work as
fertilizer.

   Mama has made me an appointment with a skin
doctor to get them BURNED off. HELP!!!!!

                          Sincerely,
                          Venola Mae
                          The most unlucky
                          person alive

Wednesday

Sally,

Yes, I do walk around barefoot, but no, I did not step in toad pee. Even if you're joking, your comment is not very funny or nice.

Sincerely,

Venola Mae Cutright

River Road
Belington, WV 26250
July 10, 1996

Mr. John Casto
Circulation Director
The Elkins Exponent
Elkins, WV 26241

Dear Mr. Casto:

My brother Bobby will be delivering my papers for a few days while I am recovering from an unfortunate illness.

I will be back by Saturday.

P.S. It is not necessary to send flowers. I just had some plantar warts removed and am having trouble walking without screaming.

P.P.S. Does this disqualify me from being nominated for paper carrier of the month?

Sincerely,

Venola Mae

Friday
July 12

Dear Sally,

Yes, I am feeling better and can walk without screaming. Thank you for asking and for not telling Missy about the W-A-R-T-S. Ugh, I can't stand to even say the word. The only thing is the doctor says I have to wear shoes and WHITE socks to cut down the chances of infection setting in. (Yes, I look like a dork AND my feet sweat, which makes them itch.)

P.S. Sammy Potter is the stupidest paper carrier alive. I have recently found out he only delivers half his route, randomly, before burying the leftovers in the Hi/Lo Dumpster.

I told Mama and Daddy, and they said Potter kids never have been known for their smarts. Daddy went on to say that when you hear that last name, you can pretty near bet on the phrases "good for nothin' " or "never amount to much" being next in line.

Mama said I couldn't tell anyone that he said

this, so I have to swear you to secrecy. Okay?

Sammy is <u>sure</u> to get in trouble soon. First, the customers are sure to complain to his parents and to Mr. Casto, the head of the circulation department, and second and even more stupid, Sammy is the same as throwing extra Fudgsicle and Fire Stix money in the Dumpster. Each one of those undelivered, thrown-away papers is worth 6½ cents credit to us <u>EXPO</u> newspaper deliverers.

Last week I started circling around after my route and searching through the Hi/Lo's bin for Sammy's rejects. I tear off the "EXPO" from each <u>Elkins Exponent</u>, and this will bring in an extra four or five dollars a week.

Mr. Casto may wonder why I had so many unsold newspaper credits this week, but he never said anything, since none of my customers complained of not getting their papers.

How are you and A.J. getting along??? Is Missy's poison ivy better????? Write me soon. This makes three letters to your two in a week. Where are you??????????

P.P.S. Do you think Sammy is cute, and would you ever like him?

Circle at least one:
   Yes, like Brad Pitt
   Yes, like a puppy

No, you're nuts
No, you're disgusting
No, I've gone to throw up

Sincerely,

Venola Mae

```
   2 soon
+ 2 be
─────────
   4 gotten by you
```

Monday

Dear Sally,

You're not going to believe what Mama did! She signed me up to deliver a paper to the FUNERAL HOME! Help!!!

Remember how I told you I was getting lots of new customers? Well, things have got out of hand. I started out with 37, but now I'm up to 78! I guess word is getting around how dependable I am at getting the papers delivered <u>every</u> day, unlike someone we both know, and for some reason people like this.

Now I'm begging Mama not to answer the phone anymore. "Let it ring, Mama. I know it's another little old lady at the top of the highest peak in town asking 'Can that sweet little Venola Mae start bringing me a daily? I'd like to have it by 4:00 before "Oprah" comes on, if she can manage. I'll give her a nickel extra a week to bring mine first.'"

That's what Miss Wilma Facemeir asked when she called from the funeral home. Mama said,

"Oh, of course, Miss Wilma, that wouldn't be out of Venola Mae's way at all, and we wouldn't hear of you giving her a cent extra. No, I insist—that's her job. She'll start tomorrow, unless you want her to run over with one of her extras from today."

Of course, I knew exactly where Miss Wilma lived, and when I heard Mama saying that it wasn't out of my way, I started waving my arms and shaking my head, but I guess Mama's not any good at playing charades or sign language because she just swatted at me with a newspaper and kept on yakking with Miss Wilma.

I especially wasn't crazy about the idea of delivering a paper to a funeral home, but what Miss Wilma wants I see that she is going to get.

I'll let you know what it's like after I deliver the first paper tomorrow—if I don't chicken out or get killed by a ghost.

Sincerely,

V. M. Cutright

Your best friend

2 young
+2 die
4 a stupid paper route

River Road
Belington, WV 26250
July 15, 1996

Mr. John Casto
Circulation Director
The Elkins Exponent
Elkins, WV 26241

Dear Mr. Casto:

URGENT REPLY REQUESTED

Can a mama make a paper carrier deliver a
paper even to a house she doesn't want to? Let me
know—SOON! PLEASE!

Sincerely,

V. M.

Wednesday

Dear Sally,

I lived! All the way up the hill to the funeral home, I kept imagining what it was going to be like. I was expecting the sky to turn dark and lightning and thunder, just like outside Chilly Billy's castle on "Monsterpiece Theatre."

But the sun kept shining, and I threw the paper up the stairs and ran.

P.S. The only person I saw—LIVE OR DEAD— was Monroe Streets. He is the funeral home caretaker, and he was waxing the hearse in the front yard. I think the sound of the paper whizzing through the air and smacking the front door about gave him a heart attack. I guess anyone would be kind of jumpy working with dead people all day.

Venola

  2 silly
+2 jump to conclusions
  4 watching monster movies

Come home soon!!!!!!!!!!!

Friday

Dear Sally,

Going to the funeral home has been pretty much the same as any other delivery only with more stairs to climb, 32!!

It's not really that scary at all. It kind of reminds me of the White House with all its white columns, or the place that Samson pushed down in that Samson and Delilah movie we saw.

It's been real quiet up there, and now I try to tiptoe across the faded green artificial grass and slide the paper between the screen and main door without being noticed, but this is near to impossible when there is a funeral going on.

Like today. I positioned the paper inside the door, but to the right, behind a folding metal chair so no one would trip on it while they were grieving. I thought of this myself.

But we'll see how brave I'll be on this Saturday—COLLECTION DAY! I'll have to go inside. Wish you were here to go with me.

Aren't you tired of camp yet? What do you mean Missy's being nice to you? Be careful!

YOUR BEST FRIEND,

VENOLA

```
   2 soon
 + 2 trust
 + a spy
   4 a minute
```

River Road
Belington, WV 26250
July 20, 1996

Mr. John Casto
Circulation Director
The Elkins Exponent
Elkins, WV 26241

RE: Previous Urgent Message

Dear Mr. Casto:

Never mind about that last letter I sent you.
False alarm. Miss Wilma is not too bad.

Sincerely,

Venola Mae

Saturday!

Dear Sally,

The scariest part about collecting was going down the dark hall and up the poorly lit stairs to where Miss Wilma lives. Yet I knew if I wanted my money I had to collect. So I went inside and up the maroon-carpeted stairs (which reminded me of dried blood) to the apartment above.

Maybe because of all those reruns of the "Munsters" and "Addams Family," I expected to be attacked by Mr. and Mrs. Funeral Home Parlor, complete with black capes, pale faces, and fangs. But it was nothing like Chilly Billy's dusty old cob-webbed castle.

Once upstairs, everything smelled like lemon Pledge and brownies, and I didn't even have to knock. The door to the apartment was open, and there in a La-Z-Boy recliner was Miss Wilma chuckling away at "Gilligan's Island" and munching on a Jolly Rancher Fire Stix (the 15-cent kind) which, as you know, are both particular favorites of mine!

Most customers leave you standing outside even in rainstorms while they count their pennies rather than have you track up their welcome mats or run the chance of you stealing a knickknack, but Miss Wilma pulled me in and sat me down in front of her 25″ color television set, showed me how to use the lever on the recliner, and tossed me her remote. She said to make myself comfortable and have a Fire Stix while she found her purse and the 65 cents she owed.

The whole time Miss Wilma was down the hall, she was asking me about school, the paper route, my family, and about everything else all at once.

"What are you doing delivering papers instead of being down at the picture show with all the other kids? Papers will wait. Movies, now, are another story, they go ahead and start without you, and if you're like me, if you miss that first couple of minutes, you're lost and never able to catch up," Miss Wilma called out from somewhere down the hall.

But before I could tell her that it was the same "Rocky" movie as last week, Miss Wilma had changed the subject and moved on to analyzing my genealogy.

"Now, let's see, you're Marie Hanson's daughter, aren't you? Good speller, that Marie. We went all the way to the state championship, too, and she would have won if I had just remembered to teach her <u>pneumonia</u>. That disease with its silent 'p' is a killer. Can you spell it?"

She didn't give me a chance to show off and show her that I could. She started screaming the letters down the hall at the top of her lungs. "P-N-E-U-M-O-N-I-A. Pneumonia."

"Gilligan's Island" went off before Miss Wilma found her purse, so I was getting ready to tell her that she could wait until the next week to pay me. Then I heard a hoot of success, and down the hall she came.

When Miss Wilma dropped the coins in my hand, a roll of cherry Life Savers clunked with them!

"Would you mind awfully eating those? I like <u>strawberry</u>, not cherry, but try telling my ignorant brother that. When he goes to the store for me, he must wear a blindfold," she complained.

I told her I could sure sympathize with anyone with a stupid brother, and said that she was lucky to have only one. Then I admitted that I couldn't really tell the difference between cherry and strawberry Life Savers.

"Well, then, your taste buds are lazy," she said. "We'll have to do something about waking them up."

As I started down the stairs, Miss Wilma called,

"You tell that mother and father of yours to come and see me sometime. You all live over on the River Road, don't you? That's not too far."

I'm glad Miss Wilma is not a bloodthirsty vampire, and only an old retired schoolteacher who taught both Mama and Daddy.

She's nice, even if she used to be a T-E-A-C-H-E-R. I think you're going to like her—that is, if you're not chicken to go inside an old dark three-storey funeral home.

Got to go. Supper's ready!

Come home soon,

Venola Mae

Paper Girl Extroidinaire
(sp? I can't find my dictionary.)

Wednesday
July 24

Dear Sally,

I think Miss Wilma might be lonely. She loves to entertain kids like me with her stories and hates funeral parlors and their musty smells as much as the next person, except her brother owns one and lets her live in the apartment for just utilities.

He lives in that big old mansion across the street, but I don't deliver over there because he is cheap and reads Miss Wilma's paper after she is done with it.

I've been spending lots of hours with her this week. Most of the time I forget that she is 84 and that we are sitting on top of a funeral parlor. Her eyes sparkle more than her bright-colored striped and flowered tank tops when she tells me about the latest argument she's had with her brother.

Just yesterday she said, "I tell him all the time that his cronies will never get their hands on me. I won't allow that old weasel-faced Monroe Streets to touch my body while I am alive, and believe me he has tried, and I sure enough refuse to let him ogle and dress me up in only the Lord knows what once I'm dead."

I've never heard any of our teachers talk like this before. All Miss Montgomery ever says is "Venola Mae, please go to the board and conjugate 'to be,' " or "Venola Mae, is that gum you're cracking?" She never tells any funny stories on herself and never gets half as excited as Miss Wilma unless you count the time Sammy set off that stink bomb in the bathroom.

Every afternoon we drink iced lemonade and Miss Wilma tells me about her past, the latest town gossip, and a lot of other stuff I've never heard of before.

Can't wait for you to meet her. Are you sure Missy isn't up to something? Maybe she's just trying to get you to let your guard down and then she'll try to steal A.J. again.

Sincerely,

V. M.

Thursday
July 25

Dear Sally,

I don't know if I can take it anymore! After Daddy and Mama have spent near a hundred dollars on my feet, those warts and some other ones have popped out before the burnt places have even quit hurting all the way.

I haven't even walked on the ground barefoot in weeks. Yet them warts keep coming. Every night I count them like I used to count pennies in my piggy bank. "Fifteen, sixteen, seventeen, eighteen," I count and know that my entire body from toe to head will be one big wart by the time the summer is over.

Miss Wilma has a home remedy for wart removal that she says won't cost me a dime. She says, "Touch a new penny to each wart, bundle them all up, and toss them in the road. Whoever finds them gets your warts." That couldn't work, could it?

She gave me a roll of pennies for the cure, but I

couldn't stand the thought of throwing my bad luck, or all those pennies, onto someone else. Instead, I bought me some Wise barbecued potato chips and tried to eat away my depression.

I might as well be fat AND warty.

Sally, will you still be my friend even if I start looking worse than Chilly Billy's creature from the black lagoon?

Unfortunately,

Venola Mae Creature

River Road
Belington, WV 26250
July 26, 1996

Imperial Magic Sea Monkey Company
P.O. Box 2000
Destin, FL 32541

Dear Sea Monkey People:

   It's me again, and the monkeys just aren't making it. Is there something you're forgetting to tell me? Do you think it would help if I put them in a little tank with a filter and a light? They are on sale at Wal-Mart for $9.99.

   Let me know what you think. I might try it soon anyway because what do I have to lose?

                              Sincerely,

                              Venola Mae

Saturday
July 27

Dear Sally,

I need your opinion a.s.a.p. Do you think I should become an accountant?

Miss Wilma says, "Yes, that's a good career for you. I've noticed how fast you figure numbers. No matter what combination I give you, you always give the right change."

But then again, it's not real hard to count to 65 cents, is it?

Miss Wilma wishes she would have had the chance to become an accountant instead of a teacher, but I think she made the right choice, because counting money is not her specialty.

Sometimes we stack up my coins from the route across her table—pennies, dimes, and nickels in stacks of ten, and quarters in stacks of four—and then we put them in rolls. But when I go home, I have to double-check because when she gets wound up with one of her stories, she stuffs some extra coins in.

(Recounting has paid off, 34 cents so far!)

But after talking with Miss Wilma, I could understand why she might have liked to try something else besides teaching. She's so inquisitive she'd have made a great detective or archeologist or maybe even a famous talk show host.

Miss Wilma told me that she only had two choices back then—nursing or teaching. "I simply couldn't stand the sight of blood or the smell of sick people—or their whining—so teaching it was," she said. I always wondered why people became teachers.

Would you pick nursing or teaching? I bet nursing. I think I would of cut my hair short and pretended to be a man, so I could of become a famous war correspondent, detective, or a mystery writer or something.

P.S. No, Miss Wilma is not a boring old woman. She is lots of fun—just like a kid. Got to go. Mama is yelling for me to come to the store with her. Bobby needs to punch in by 5:00, or he will be in trouble again.

See ya soon,

Venola Mae

Sunday
July 28

Dear Sally,

HAVE YOU HEARD???? Today our church was robbed at gunpoint by three unidentified people who the police haven't caught yet.

I think I can identify at least two of them!!! At the time I didn't know them from Adam, with their masks, shotguns, and dark clothes. (I don't know why they chose dark turtlenecks for a Sunday morning service. I guess too many gangster movies.)

Those masked men busting in and interrupting Reverend Lawson's sermon was scarier than last year's play when Jesus walked down the aisle in the dark, dragging and banging his wooden cross. Almost as many of the kids were crying this time, too.

They made us put our purses, wallets, and jewelry in clothes baskets as they walked down the aisle. One of the robbers stayed by the door. Then they all backed out, taking our belongings with them.

My family says we're going next Sunday, even though we never got any of our stuff back, but I'm not—even if they return my pinky ring. They can just forget it!

Mama says, "Preparation of religious life for the next world is like studying for a test and doing homework—if you try to do it at the last minute, you'll fail." But you know I've always been good at last-minute cramming, and I'm willing to take my chances again.

Daddy says religion will help you through the worst, but to tell you the truth, when those guys in masks with shotguns burst through those double doors, I would have given up religion in a heartbeat to have been anywhere but in that church.

To be transported to Anna Mae's Pool Hall would have been the best thing on this earth. Not that I drink, but I might have given it a whirl.

I should have known it was somebody pretty stupid when they chose OUR church to rob. The Presbyterian or even the United Methodist would have brought in a lot more contributions. The Blessed Baptist Ministry is not a wealthy church, and everyone in town knows it.

Remember last summer when some sinner took the liberty of adding the words "S&H Greenstamps" underneath the "Jesus Saves" messages on both sides of the bus. Maybe it was the same hoodlums that robbed us. Maybe they've just got it in for Baptists.

They didn't even pick a good Sunday to rob us, like Easter or Christmas. According to Ancil Teter, this week's counter, we only had 34 members present, but he isn't really sure because he didn't get a chance to do his usual double check. Mama says that the reason he counts twice is because he's not real good with math, and if he doesn't get the same number twice, the Reverend just takes an average. I didn't know that, did you?

Why would anyone pick July 28? They could of at least waited until the pension checks came out. What's another week or so?

Stupid, that's the only excuse I can come up with. That's what makes me think that Sammy Potter was the mastermind behind the whole thing. He already has a record. He still has a month's probation from where him and his brother stole that 4 × 4 Jeep and pulled kids up the hill after they rode their sleds to the bottom until someone called the police. Daddy still shakes his head when we go up that hill and says it was a wonder someone wasn't run over or killed.

Sammy may have spent the LAST of his numerous junior high years rolling back his eyelids and wiggling his tongue at us girls. (And he wondered why he couldn't get a date to the end-of-the-year dance!)

Now get this. I think his church-robbing accomplice was Tommy Flint. Yep, King Apricot himself. And he just broke his own record the week before school was out by eating seventy-two during fifth-period lunch. Mine was one of the apricots that scored him the title back in January, remember? Who would have thought that my innocent generosity and his lunchroom pigginess would lead to a life of crime? Just think, before the apricots, all he was famous for was swallowing wads of paper the size of 50-cent pieces. Soon Mrs. Gump will be putting their pictures up down at the post office—that is, if they try to run when I turn them in. I wonder if they know I'm on to them?

The phone's ringing. Maybe it's some news, the police, or even a reporter! I'll be back in a minute.

Nope. It was just Reverend Lawson. He told Mama it's our Christian duty to come back to services next Sunday. He's calling around town promising a humdinger of a sermon on "Thou Shalt Not Steal," but I'd just the same Mama videotape it for me.

Why should I go to all the trouble of putting on a dress and rolling up my hair the night before on orange juice cans just to get shot? No thanks.

After all, what's to say that the third gangster won't return to the scene of the crime even after I turn in Sammy and Tommy? Reverend Lawson says his brother Marvin, the deputy, will stand guard at the door, but I just don't know if my heart could get into praying, knowing that there's a man at the door protecting us from gunfire. Sally, you could write Mama and vouch for me. You've heard the teachers tell me my concentration ain't that hot.

Why does God's house need Marvin Lawson's protection anyway? Why didn't God just let them have it with a thunderbolt or two for even thinking about robbing Him? Maybe He figured that their own guilt would eat away at them and be a far greater lesson. Sammy? Fat chance! God's a lot more understanding than I am; that's probably why I'm not in charge of lightning bolts.

I never thought I'd have a barrel of a gun waved in my face. I'm not really what anyone would call a risktaker, am I? I don't walk late at night by myself, cross the street before the light turns, or eat too many Vienna sausages. So why should I risk sudden death by going to church?

Anyway, I'm thinking of converting. On "Donahue" last week they had this doctor from India who told all about how to live for a long time. He said if we spend our lives in fear, it will speed up the aging process and that we must shed our need for approval. Well, he might not have come right out and said, "Venola Mae, don't go to church and you'll live longer," but he definitely implied it, and I'm sure he would take my side if he knew the circumstances.

So today I shed my "need for parental approval" and came right out and told Mama that Melvin, Katrina, and Bobby could have the whole backseat to themselves on the way to church, that I had decided to stay at home and observe the Sabbath in my own way.

Mama fumed, saying a few choice words that she might need to go to church and apologize for, but I still believe I have a right to my own decision. And so does Katrina, especially since she's always complaining that by the time she gets to church her dress needs re-ironed because of my hogging up so much room. (And we all know that Katrina's rear is bigger than mine.)

It's not like I'm planning to sit at home all day Sunday sewing on a king-size quilt or something. Who would dare do that after hearing for the last eleven years that the devil would make you pull out each and every stitch with your teeth? Not that I understand what the big deal is with sewing on Sunday. (I think it's just an old tale started by somebody who didn't like to sew.)

I tried to expand Mama's sewing rule a couple of weeks ago, and I told Mama that I probably shouldn't wash the Sunday dishes either, or the devil might make me wash and dry each one with my tongue someday. She told me that if I didn't get my hands in the dishpan, I would be washing them with my smart-mouthed tongue faster than I thought, and threatened to wash my mouth out with Ivory liquid right there on the spot.

Mama's not much of a diplomat, but I'm not planning on backing down next Sunday. It's not just the robbery. I've been having my doubts about organized religion for a long time, at least for the last month. That's when Reverend Lawson started in on MTV and some of our favorite TV shows.

He said, "Parents, you need to take control of the remote. Save your children. We all know that the devil controls the airwaves." I only wanted to ask how if the devil controlled the airwaves, how all those religious shows like "The Power Team" and "The 700 Club" found their way into our home via the TV. Wouldn't the devil block them airwaves just out of meanness? But Mama had seen me fidgeting in my seat and grabbed my hand before I got it raised high enough to be seen from the pulpit.

For even thinking about bothering Reverend

Lawson during services, she made me give up one whole week of television, except for PBS. Sometimes I wonder just whose side the reverend is on, don't you? I know it's not mine because he complimented Mama on her "strong parental discipline." I think he just wants bigger tips in the collection plate.

Another thing that made me kind of lose faith was Fay Rhodes. I prayed for someone to catch her after she stole my black patent-leather dress shoes during gym class last May. She said they were hers and never got struck by lightning. I've been watching them at church every week as the scuff marks just keep adding up, and now it's too late for anything to be done anyway. I should have just stolen them back, but I knew that somehow Reverend Lawson and Mama would get dragged into the middle, and I would probably just lose some more of my favorite TV shows and be sentenced to more public television for causing trouble and not being "giving" enough.

I don't know if I'll ever convince Mama to let me miss church, but I know I could be of more help at home. I could go through my yearbooks and try to pick out some suspects for that other unidentified robber. He was bigger—maybe it was DeWayne Chidester. He's always in the principal's office for acting up and stealing chalk and erasers and stuff. Or maybe Robert Huffman. He always seems up to no good. So you see, with my inside information, my talents are being wasted.

If I could just convince Mama of that. Yeah, I know. See you at church.

P.S. Ask your mama if you have to go to church. Maybe we can camp out instead.

Venola Mae
Crime Solver

P.P.S. Am I too young for the witness protection program they talk about on "Unsolved Mysteries"?

P.P.P.S. Will you go with me if I have to change my identity and move to California or somewhere? We could tell people we are sisters. I would dye my hair blonde like yours. Or would you rather make yours brown???????

P.P.P.P.S. OUCH! I HAVE TO STOP WRITING OR MY HAND MIGHT FALL OFF!

River Road
Belington, WV 26250
July 29, 1996

Unsolved Mysteries
P.O. Box 11449
Burbank, CA 91510–1449

Dear Mr. Robert Stack:

  Our church was robbed yesterday, and I was
hoping you could help. Mrs. Gump down at the
post office did me a big favor and made a Xerox
copy of a letter that I wrote to my friend Sally. I
think this information might help you crack the
case.
  Thanks.
  P.S. Please don't arrest Mrs. Gump for using the
post office copy machine to photocopy my letter. It
would have taken me too long to write the whole
letter again—plus I have a blister on my writing
finger! (Anyway, Mrs. Gump says I am one of
Uncle Sam's best customers, and she doesn't think
he'll get mad about a few free copies.)

P.P.S. I really love your show and watch it EVERY Friday night! Do you have any free T-shirts?

Sincerely,

Venola Mae Cutright

A Concerned Citizen and Fellow Crime Solver

River Road
Belington, WV 26250
July 30, 1996

Mr. John Casto
Circulation Director
The Elkins Exponent
Elkins, WV 26241

Dear Mr. Casto:

Are you sure that the three men from Michigan you mentioned in your paper today really did rob the church? Because I kind of had a couple of others in mind.

If you find out there's been a mistake, I might be able to help.

P.S. Thank you for the second certificate. Now I have one for each end of my bed, which is good because sometimes I sleep with my head at the foot, so now I'll see a certificate either way.

Sincerely,

Venola Mae Cutright
Paper Carrier of the Month
(Two months running)

69

Tuesday

Dear Sally,

Today I told Miss Wilma that her penny wart
cure flopped.

"Maybe no one found them yet, where YOU
threw them," she answered. I could just feel guilty,
but I think SHE KNOWS what I really did with
them pennies.

"You have to believe," she said.

I am getting desperate—or is it desparate? How
can I start seventh grade with all these warts all
over my feet? I don't need Missy giving me any
new nicknames in gym class. I have a bump on
my hand, too. What if they spread to my face? I
worry and count them ten times a day.

Miss Wilma said, "Girl, you've got to do
something. The only thing that can help a case
this advanced is your mama's dirty dishrag."

I told her I wasn't rubbing that stinking thing on
my feet, and that she could wipe that idea plumb
out of her head.

"Hush!" she said. "Listen to me." Her voice was

70

low and serious, and she squeezed my warty feet between her strong hands. "If your mama finds out, it won't work. I'm not telling you to rub a dishrag on anything. You have to steal it and bury it somewhere secret without anybody seeing you."

I'll admit she convinced me for about five seconds, and then I came to. Miss Wilma is always telling me one tale or another. One day when we were out taking a walk, she spotted a robin. "Sshh, there's a robin," she whispered and started a slow count to 100. When she finished and the bird hadn't moved, she pranced around singing, "Now my wish'll come true." Which I didn't understand, because it wasn't more than two weeks before that she was telling me how unlucky a bird could be. When a bird landed on her windowsill, she slammed the window down before I had any idea what was going on, and she warned, "A bird in the house means a death in the family."

Nutty ideas like that made me not real anxious to steal anyone's dishrag—especially Mama's.

"Give me a break, Miss Wilma—this is the nineties, not the Stone Age. I go to a dermatologist," I said, which she didn't like one bit.

"Fine, you old bumpy-footed fool. Go to your fancy specialist. I can see the fine improvements that genius has made!" She dropped my feet and turned toward the kitchen. "And see if I give you any more wart money to blow on junk food."

After the short time we have known each other, she knows me TOO well.

Well, I have to go help Mama in the garden. She thinks I'm spending too much time in my room writing to you or watching repeats on TV. So she said for me to get outside and get some fresh air. (What does she think I get on my paper route?!?)

Bye for now,

Venola

2 depressed
+ 2 scream
4 help

Wednesday
July 31

Dear Sally,

I know I probably shouldn't have done it, but I'll buy Mama a three-pack of NEW dishrags for her birthday next month.

Venola Mae
"Kleptomaniac"
Cutright

P.S. Am I awful?

Wednesday
letter no. 2

Dear Sally,

Found a packet of seeds today as I was walking by the junior high. I think they might be marijuana!!!! I showed them to Miss Wilma, and she planted them purely out of what she called "curiosity and an old woman's longing for a little scientific research."

She buried them in potting soil in ice trays out on her sunporch, just so we can watch them grow—more as a joke than anything else—NOT TO ACTUALLY SMOKE!!! They are probably not what we think.

Congratulations on winning the camp swimming title again this year!

P.S. No, I don't think I'm spending too much time with Miss Wilma. You will understand once you meet her.

Venola

Friday

Dear Sally,

Would you ever go skinny-dipping?!? I wouldn't never. Yeah, I know I can't swim, but how am I supposed to learn when Mama makes me promise not to go near the water till I know how to swim?

The reason I'm asking is because I know someone who did. Guess who. Miss Wilma!!!! Not recently, but when she was a teacher she went skinny-dipping. (I told you she is not a boring old lady!)

She said that she went to a roadhouse (I think it's a bar) with some other teachers, mostly women, and they went skinny-dipping to protest their rights to privacy.

Miss Wilma said, "We just did it to tick off that nosy superintendent. He thought he could rule the women teachers' lives, while the men could do whatever with whomever they chose. We all started off drinking tall lemonades until Ocie Lou Yaterman started flirting with the bartender. Then he gave us bourbon and rum. It was a kind of strike, only we didn't have signs. After a while we didn't even have clothes." She laughed and said, "Oh, but did we know how to have fun."

Can you believe it? Do you think our parents ever skinny-dipped? Do you think Miss Montgomery ever skinny-dipped? Ahhhhhhh, I can't stand to think about it. See drawing below. I call it "Miss Montgomery loses her mind."

Venola
The artist extraordinaire

76

Saturday

Dear Sally,

I've got some gossip that tops even skinny-dipping, but you have to swear not to tell ANYONE!

Miss Wilma told me that one time she had a two-week marriage to a traveling salesman. After that, it was annulled. (Like a divorce.)

She says everyone in town has always wondered what happened, and that I'm the only one privileged enough (& now you) to know the details that the rest of the town has to guess about, especially the part about meeting him twenty years later in a bus station and what they said and done.

I'd tell you now, but I'm sworn to secrecy, and we wouldn't want this to fall into the wrong hands (M-I-S-S-Y)—or Mrs. Gump down at the post office, so I'll tell you someday soon IN PERSON.

Let me just say that the Elkins Expo would pay top dollar for this exclusive.

FOURTEEN days until we are together again.

Your gossip connection,

Venola "Scoop" Cutright

        2 good of friends
      + 2 keep secrets
      ―――――――――――
        4 very long

P.S. Forget what I told you about Sammy and Tommy. Marvin Lawson says those other guys they caught confessed.

Tuesday
August 6

Dear Sally,

I CAN'T believe that you went skinny-dipping with Missy and the other Jackals. Sorry you got in trouble, IF you're telling me the truth.

Sincerely,

Venola

Thursday

Dear Touchy Sally,

No, I did not mean to call you a liar. I was just kidding. Write me.

Saturday
August 10

Dear Sally,

No, it wasn't your fault. I shouldn't have
questioned your honesty. I'm sorry you are having
a bad week, and I'm sorry you broke up with A.J.
And yes, I forgive you for being touchy.

P.S. I told you Missy was evil. See drawing.

Your best friend,

Venola

$$\begin{array}{r} 2 \text{ friends} \\ +\,2 \text{ sorry} \\ \hline 4 \text{ words} \end{array}$$

Dear Sally,

NEWS FLASH!!! Here's something that will cheer
you up. I received my JCPenney's catalog today,
and I checked with your mama, and she promised
to order your copy today. She said the flower shop
has been swamped with funerals and weddings
this month and she hasn't had a second of free
time for anything. But don't worry, I'll remind her
again tomorrow, and it will be here by the time
you get home.

It won't be long until we can camp out in
Bobby's tent and pick which models are the
prettiest and dream about all the school clothes
we wish we could order—just like last year.

P.S. If someone at camp has a catalog, look at
page 318 Items C, D, & E. I would order dark
green to match my eyes. What do you think? Do
you like them? Would it make me look taller and
geekier, or is this not even possible? Be honest,
would I look stupid in them? I usually don't like

dresses, but that one is really cute with the little vest and matching belt.

Venola

Sunday
August 11

Dear Sally,

Had the same dream again. One where the robbers come in and start down the hall of our trailer. I keep hearing shots and I know they are shooting my family and putting them in coffins, but I can't move, and then they get to me, and the gun won't shoot. It just clicks in my ear. Click. Click. (The robbers get really mad and try another gun. Click. Click.) Then I wake up shaking.

Mama says I can sleep with a light on if I want, but who could sleep with a light on?

I'm not sure I want to sleep out in the tent like we did last year.

Venola

Monday

Dear Sally,

The seeds that Miss Wilma planted are starting to shoot up. They look like tiny tomato plants or palm trees. I believe they are really marijuana plants because they look just like the picture in our health book.

Venola

Tuesday
August 13

Dear Sally,

Marvin Lawson, the deputy sheriff, showed up at Miss Wilma's last night around 10:00 to "investigate a complaint." Miss Wilma said he knocked on her door and made her hand over all of our plants, but I think he mostly came for some of her cookies. He, like everyone else in town, is one of her former students, and he was real polite and laughed while he was scolding her. However, he did threaten to read her "her rights" when she told him that they were really only tomato plants and that he better not lay a finger on them or her.

When he left with our plants, she asked him to turn on his blue lights and shine his spotlight all around the house, "just to give the neighbors a little something extra to talk about. I want them to get their money's worth, since they're wasting tax dollars making you drive up here." Then she gave him a Ziploc bag full of chocolate chip cookies and TWO Fire Stixs "for the road."

Mr. Lawson said he would, and she says as he pulled out he even let his siren squawk a little.

Although we don't know for sure who told, Miss Wilma blames Mrs. Gump, who lives just two houses away. I tend to agree, but Miss Wilma has told half the town what she was growing, so I guess it could of been anyone.

See ya soon.

Venola Mae

$$\begin{array}{r} 4 \text{ days} \\ -\ 2 \text{ go until} \\ \hline 2 \text{ friends reunite!!} \end{array}$$

Wednesday
August 14

Dear Sally,

Miss Wilma received a combination "apology/thank-you-for-the-cookies" card from Marvin Lawson. The plants really were little tomatoes.

She wrote him back to stop by for more cookies anytime, but not to come for one of her special tomato and mayonnaise sandwiches on rye bread unless he supplied the tomatoes.

P.S. I miss you, too. But it won't be long now!

Venola

River Road
Belington, WV 26250
August 14, 1996

Imperial Magic Sea Monkey Company
P.O. Box 2000
Destin, FL 32541

Dear Sea Monkey People:

Nothing happened again. Are you sure the ones you're sending me haven't already been cremated?

If they have, you are being kind of mean. Maybe Mr. Bookout's practical jokes are rubbing off on you.

Please send me some LIVE monkeys. I promise to pay you the shipping if you tell me how much.

Sincerely,

Venola

Wednesday, late
August 14

Dear Sally,

   Why didn't YOU tell me you aren't coming straight home from camp? It was awful to hear the news from a complete stranger!!!

   Bobby said your mama went through his checkout line today at Shop-N-Save, and she told him that you are going to your grandparents until right before school starts. IS THIS TRUE?!?

   He said she gave you the choice of working in the flower shop with her, staying with a baby-sitter, or visiting the grandparents, and that YOU CHOSE the grandparents.

   Why?!? You should have told me and maybe I could have talked her into you staying with us if she didn't want you staying alone all day. Or Miss Wilma would have probably let you stay with her. Now we won't have any free time to spend together this summer.

Venola Mae Cutright
Your BEST Friend?????

```
  2 shocked
+ 2 hurt
  4 not knowing
```

P.S. You're not taking Missy with you, are you??? I don't think your grandparents would like her.

P.P.S. Is there anything else you are forgetting to tell me?

Thursday
August 15

Dear Sally,

GUESS WHAT!?!?!?!

I'm going on vacation to SEA WORLD!!!! Too bad you decided to visit your grandparents because we could have picked you up on the last day of camp.

My aunt and uncle and cousins from Parkersburg are coming to get me, and I'll be gone Saturday and Sunday. Even though it takes only five hours to get there, we're staying all night at their house in Parkersburg on the way back.

(Bobby says he'll deliver my papers on Saturday before he goes to work at Shop-N-Save IF I pay him five dollars AND buy him a Sea World souvenir. Brothers! It's highway robbery, but I've got to pay it, or I won't get to go. Bobby won't even have time to collect because he has to be at work by four, but I can do that Monday when I get back. OR if people will pay early, I can spend some of the money on Shamu the Killer Whale T-shirts and stuff.)

P.S. What is your favorite color (of T-shirt)? Pick two or three in case they don't have your first choice.

blue
black
white
green
red (yuck)
yellow
purple!
pink
aqua
other _____

River Road
Belington, WV 26250
August 15, 1996

Imperial Magic Sea Monkey Company
P.O. Box 2000
Destin, FL 32541

Dear Sea Monkey People:

The light isn't making the monkeys grow, but the filter is helping me sleep better. I haven't had a nightmare all week. Thanks.

Sincerely,

Venola

Mr. and Mrs. Herbert Cutright
James, Melvin, Philip, Bobby, and Katrina Cutright
River Road
Belington, WV 26250

August 17, 1996

Dear Mama, Daddy, Jim, Melvin, Phil, Bobby, and Kat,

I am having a great time. I can't believe I'm HERE! You all would like it, too. It IS NOT just for babies.
P.S. Bobby,
Thanks for delivering the papers! I would send you a separate postcard, but I spent all my money on souvenirs (Yes, I bought you something!) and snow cones. It is HOT!, and we are sitting right out in the sun waiting for Shamu the killer whale.
P.P.S. I hope Shamu doesn't splash this card. I'd write more, but I'm out of room.

V. M.

Monday
August 19

Dear Sally,

Are you having fun with your grandparents? I
hope so! I have a favor to ask. Do you think you
could teach me to swim? If so, I don't want to be
an accountant anymore. I think I want to be a
marine biologist or a barefoot water-skier. Which
do you think would be more exciting? Miss Wilma
says waterskiing might pay more, but it's like a
career in modeling, and I'll need something to fall
back on when I'm old.

I wish you could have been with us. It was
great. Melony and Teresa and Brian and I rode in
the back of their truck on these old car seats that
their dad welded down on the truck bed. Melony
and Teresa got to ride the right way because they
said they would get trucksick riding backwards,
but Melony got sick anyway.

I had almost as much fun in the truck as at Sea
World. At first Brian and I were riding near the
tailgate with the lid to the camper up and waving
at the tractor-trailers. Brian knew this way of

jerking his arm, and the truckers would smile and blow their horns. But then Aunt Dru said we had to get back up on the seat because we would get too many fumes back by the tailgate. (I think the real reason was because all the horns were making her nervous.)

Then we started singing "99 Bottles of Beer on the Wall," but Aunt Dru opened the sliding glass window on the cab of the truck again and said that we had to substitute "root beer" for "beer" or she was going to turn the truck around because she wasn't pulling into Sea World with a truckload of alcoholics.

That was the only time us kids argued on the whole trip. Melony wanted to put in "Mountain Dew," Teresa wanted to sing "one-calorie Tab" because she is on a diet, and Brian said he was going to sing "Countrytime lemonade." I wanted to sing "Sea Monkeys," but Melony said it had to be something to DRINK, so of course I chose "Dr Pepper." Which would you have picked?

P.S. I got you an aqua T-shirt. Is that okay? I hope a small will fit.

P.P.S. Do you think we could ever train fish to jump up out of the water and take food from our hands? We would get rich.

Bye for now.

Venola

Dear Sally,

I've been took!

Miss Wilma gave me a zoology book because she thinks marine biology is a good career choice. And in there it says that sea monkeys are really brine shrimp that have "flatlike legs and tails, and even under optimal (best) conditions only grow to a half inch long." THEY WILL NEVER GROW GOLDEN CROWNS OR LOOK LIKE THE PICTURES IN THE MAGAZINE!

I can't decide what to do. Mama says write and ask for my money back again, but I'm thinking about turning those Magic Sea Monkey Crooks into "Consumer Crackdown." If they investigate them, I would win $50. Would that be like ratting on them?

P.S. I wasn't saying you probably got fat at

camp. I was saying that Sea World skimps on material and that a small is really small!!!

Sincerely,

V. M.

P.P.S. I can't believe you're FINALLY coming home. Want to go on my route with me next Saturday? You would get the chance to meet Miss Wilma. She says she will make enough brownies for a real homecoming party!

River Road
Belington, WV 26250
August 19, 1996

Imperial Magic Sea Monkey Company
P.O. Box 2000
Destin, FL 32541

Dear "Sea Monkey" People:

You better sit down because I've got some BAD news for you. Your sea monkeys are not monkeys at all. They are really BRINE SHRIMP EGGS! I found this out in a zoology encyclopedia that says they are really from the genus Artemia, AND I checked with Mr. Bookout who I saw at Shop-N-Save yesterday.

Please send my money back. You don't have to send shipping and handling because at least you helped me sleep better by suggesting the light and filter. And I can use those again because I am buying a yellow tang at the LOCAL pet store. (The same pet store that sells brine shrimp eggs for

$2.00 instead of your $10.00 PLUS shipping and handling!)

P.S. Would you get mad if I gave your name to "Consumer Crackdown"? If you haven't heard of "Consumer Crackdown," it is this national television show that exposes advertising scams. I would win $50.

Sincerely,

Venola Mae Cutright

Tuesday
August 20

Dear Sally,

MY WARTS ARE GONE!!!
You're not going to believe this, but I'm telling
you any how.

A couple of weeks ago I was making raspberry
Kool-Aid (we were out of strawberry) and smelled
something sauerkraut rotten in the sink. "Steal
your mama's rag, and when it rots, your warts will
go away" started going through my head.

I was really doing Mama a favor anyway. That
rag needed thrown away years ago, so I put it out
of its misery and gave it a decent burial under the
porch, piling rock after rock on top of it and
HOPING that nobody smelled it.

Maybe I was desperate. I was getting sick of
Bobby calling me Toad Piss whenever Mama
wasn't around.

Maybe with Sea World and stuff that's why I
never noticed my warts retreating. Then today, I
noticed my foot didn't catch when I dragged it
across the coffee table.

I'm not telling anyone else but Miss Wilma about the R-A-G theft because I do not want to jinx the cure. You better not tell neither because if you do, you might be sporting around some plantar warts of your own. You never can tell with these things!

Sincerely,

Venola Mae
The Wartless Wonder

P.S. I wonder if Miss Wilma has a cure that would make people disappear. List of people to disappear: (1) Missy. (2) Sammy—for teasing me all the time. (3) Bobby—if he doesn't quit calling me names. (4) A.J., or have you forgiven him again?

P.P.S. I've got to go. We are going to Stuart's Park for a family picnic. I would write more on the way, but Mama thinks I need to "interact" and play ball with the gargoyles. (Ha! Ha!) Did I tell you that Bobby has started calling me Penhead because sometimes I forget I have a pen behind my ear?

$$\begin{array}{r} 2 \text{ happy and} \\ + 2 \text{ grateful} \\ \hline 4 \text{ words} \end{array}$$

Wednesday
August 21

Dear Sally,

The picnic was okay. We played volleyball—
EVEN Mama and Daddy! But I need to tell you
something because I'm not sure what to think or
who to believe anymore. I apologize if I gross you
out. If you get sick, just quit reading this letter at
any time and I will understand.

Remember how I told you about Miss Wilma
and her fights with her brother? Well, they're at it
again.

The main problem is Mr. Facemeir believes he
is providing what he calls "an invaluable,
necessary service for the community." His motto is
"Funerals are for the living, too!" and he is always
telling Miss Wilma, "Viewing the body and seeing
it look <u>natural</u> allows for a healthy grieving period
so that the living can get on with the here and

now"—which might be okay if he would stop there. But no, he ends every argument with, "It would just break my heart to know that you begrudged me my right to mourn, and I didn't get to prepare you a proper open-casket funeral, Sister. I want to send you off right."

But this Saturday morning before my collecting time, he added, "And anyway, what do you care what they do with you? You're just being your usual selfish self. You'll be dead." So by the time I got there for my visit, she was properly riled and ready to cause a few funerals herself.

"He wants to stretch me out for the whole world to see," Miss Wilma said. "My will specifically states that I want cremated, but he'll find a way around it. He doesn't care about my wishes. To think of people walking up and whispering, 'Oh, doesn't she look good? So young. So peaceful. So, so NATURAL!' " The way she puckered up her face was hilarious.

"I'LL BE DEAD! Who cares how natural you look when you're dead? Some of the regular funeral goers, like that gossiping Ora Miller and Joan Cruthers, haven't come to visit me in years. Why come to see me dead? Those squinty-eyed birds are always looking for a reason to flock. Do you think I'm going to provide an afternoon of entertainment for them??? I bet they haven't missed a funeral in twenty years! I'll take my flowers while I'm alive to enjoy them, thank you. If you bring me flowers when I'm dead, Venola Mae Cutright, I'll come back and kick your rump! The florists and the undertakers are the only ones who make out at funerals!"

Something told me we wouldn't be watching "Gilligan's Island" on her 25"-color screen this particular afternoon unless she cooled down, so I said, "I'm sure Mr. Facemeir just loves you and wants to know you will receive the best possible care, Miss Wilma"—which was definitely the most stupid thing I could possibly say, and I knew so before I got it all out. It set her off again for ten or fifteen minutes of ranting without breaks for breathing.

"Oh you're sure, are you? Do you understand what 'Best possible care' means to an undertaker? First, it means 'Most expensive,' and second, it means 'Most disgusting.' Embalming doesn't work like spraying Pam on a skillet or like pickling eggs by dunking them in beet juice and vinegar. They slice you with a knife and drain your blood into a big vat and pump in chemicals to match your natural coloring—maybe I should let them do it, and request a nice Coppertone suntan color. It'd be my first. I always burnt and peeled on vacations!"

I couldn't believe what she was saying, and I was ready to argue. "There's no way anyone would go to all that trouble."

"Oh, honey, that's just the beginning. That's the easy part." She was on a roll. "They scrub you, set your hair, do your nails, place your hands in the 'Rest in Peace' gesture—sometimes they have to sew them in that position. It's the best makeover you'll ever get. They apply makeup and spray glue your eyelids down, sew your lips together so your mouth doesn't fall open and look like you're snoring during the service, and if you're bucktoothed like poor old Burley Hutzler, they polish the ones that hang out and paint them with clear nail polish to make them nice and shiny!"

I think she was sorry that she'd said all she did once she saw the look on my face. I could of used a little of that artificial coloring pumping through my own veins. The thought of them subjecting my dead grandma or granddaddy or my little sister to this kind of process made me want to hit someone or something, so I started throwing rubber-banded papers at lamps and coatracks. Not too many because Miss Wilma was fast and grabbed me, trying to calm me by saying, "I was just carrying on. I didn't mean to scare you. You know how I exaggerate, Venola Mae!" She was trying to sound all cheerful, but I knew that what she'd spoken was the truth. Miss Wilma doesn't lie. Well, at least not to me.

> Your grossed-out
> friend,
>
> Venola Mae

2 green
+ 2 grossed out
4 words

Dear Sally,

Do you think Miss Wilma was SERIOUS???????????? Why would people do this????????????????????

Venola

Thursday
August 22

Dear Sally,

Do you think it's TOO MUCH to ask for Miss Wilma to prove what she told me. I guess I am bugging her too much, because she has threatened to leave my 65 cents on the porch banister.

Would you want to see what they do in a funeral parlor operating room? I can't help it. Maybe I'm possessed by Chilly Billy.

Sincerely,

Venola

2 curious
2 forget
+ a thing like this
4 a minute

Friday
August 23

Dear Sally,

Today was the day. Finally she took me in and showed me the tables and instruments that Monroe Streets uses to prepare the bodies. Miss Wilma made sure that there wasn't a corpse around because I don't think either of us could of handled that.

Monroe was real professional in his explanations and didn't tell his usual "dead" jokes and stories. Just last Thursday, he caught me outside and said, "Venola Mae, did I ever tell you about when I dropped poor dead Granny White off the table, and she came back to life?"

I knew he was teasing but I played along. "No, Mr. Streets, you never told me. What happened?"

"Well, she lived another five years, healthy as a horse, and when she died again, Mr. White said, 'Now, Monroe, take good care of my woman and watch you don't drop her again!' "

Monroe's a strange, strange man. But I think since he never gets called on for career days at school, he was proud to show anyone around and was on good behavior. He showed me wigs, fake arms, needles and wire thread, scalpels, forceps, pumps, and tubes. He tried to get me to step into the foot positioner, but it reminded me too much of the Salem stocks we read about last year in history class.

He pointed out his favorite injection and drainage points on a skeleton. "Most people in the business will go for the jugular, but that's too easy. I prefer the less conspicuous femoral artery, or occasionally the carotid." He said this like he'd discovered the techniques himself.

Oh, and he let me make a hand just like my own with plaster of Paris, which he uses when someone chops one off in a car wreck or something. This was super interesting, since I didn't know that plaster of Paris had any uses outside of vacation Bible school projects, did you?

Off to the left of the preparation room, a big walk-in closet was filled with racks of dark gray and blue suits with lacings up the backs. "In here's where lots of men and boys get their first suits," he said. "Families don't like to see their men and boys buried in flannel shirts and faded overalls, which is all lots of folks have."

For some reason this made me sadder than anything else.

P.S. Not that I'm sick or nothing, but after careful consideration, I have decided to get cremated.

P.P.S. You should, too.

P.P.P.S. No, I don't mean NOW!!!!!!!!!!!!!!!!

Your best friend,

Venola Mae

I miss you.

Saturday, early
August 24

Dear Sally,

My parents are being pigheaded! They say I
can't get cremated until I turn eighteen. So I guess
I have to be careful, and stay healthy, for the next
seven years or so.

Mama and Daddy don't understand all my talk
of cremation. They think I've seen something on
"20/20" or a "National Geographic" special, and
that it is just a phase. They would kill Miss Wilma
and Monroe if they ever found out they had taken
me there because already they are sick of hearing
about death and the embalming process, and they
have made me talk to Reverend Lawson, who in
turn has recommended a therapist if we ever get
the money ahead.

I don't think Mama and Daddy, or many other
people in the world for that matter, know what
really goes on. I don't think they want to. Most
folks just do what is expected—like when last
winter the doctors told us Mama's full-term

stillborn baby girl had to have a funeral and they had to borrow $3,000 to pay for a funeral complete with tombstone, miniature casket, hearse to the graveyard, all for a baby that neither of them even got to hold or touch.

Miss Wilma says funerals are a way of making undertakers richer and poor people poorer, and I believe her. That's why if my family wants to do something for me, they can sprinkle me along my route with extra helpings at Miss Wilma's and the Hi/Lo Dumpster.

Sincerely,

Venola Mae

P.S. If something SHOULD happen to me, my will is under my mattress. Would you make sure that Mama remembers it's there.

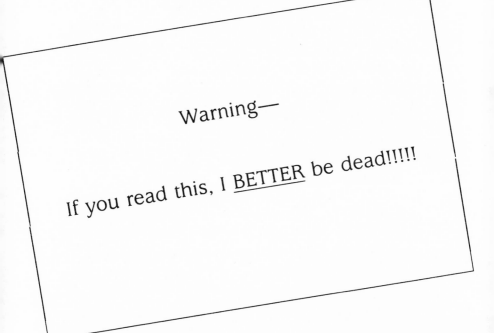

Warning—

If you read this, I <u>BETTER</u> be dead!!!!!

LAST WILL AND TESTAMENT

I, Venola Mae Cutright, being of sound mind and body, do leave the following to my friends and family:

1. The balance of my checking account ($39.15 presently) goes to my mama and daddy to be divided up amongst my four brothers and sister evenly ($7.83 each).
2. Give Sally my paperback collection, my kitten poster, AND my "Monsterpiece Theatre" T-shirt.
3. I want Sammy to have my new newspaperbag and diamond hole punchers. Also, give him my two certificates. Maybe these things will make him do a better job on his own route.
4. Mama and Daddy can sell my bike and use the money to take a vacation away from my brothers. They need it!
5. If my little sister would have lived I would have given her my sea monkeys and aquarium, but since she didn't, give them to Miss Wilma because she is awful good at growing things. And the three Jolly Rancher Fire Stix I have in my second drawer.
6. To Missy, my old warts—wherever they are. Just kidding.

Further instructions:
Please cremate me!!! I do not want to be seen with poofy funeral parlor hair. If Sammy or Missy or ANYBODY in my seventh-grade class would see me looking goofy on one of those silk pillows, I would just die.

P.S. I will come back and haunt whoever does not fulfill my last requests. I mean it.

Thursday
August 29

Miss Wilma,

I hope it's okay to write on the corner of your paper. I didn't bring any notebook paper because I thought you'd be home and I could tell you in person that Sally and I will come over at 3:30 Saturday—if that's okay.

Do you want me to bring some pop? If so, what kind?

Your best friend,

Venola

Dear Sally,

DO NOT let Mama see this! She would kill me for passing notes in church.

I stayed up real late last night wondering about you and Miss Wilma. Something tells me you didn't like her OR her stories. Why did you roll your eyes at me when she was talking?

P.S. Didn't you like her brownies?

Ven.

S,

    She isn't THAT OLD! And
who cares about that
anyway?!? I would rather talk
to her than Missy—and
sometimes you, too!!!

Y

Sally,

    I AM NOT WEIRD.

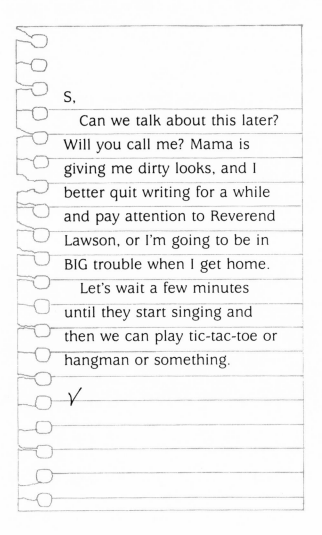

S,

Can we talk about this later?
Will you call me? Mama is
giving me dirty looks, and I
better quit writing for a while
and pay attention to Reverend
Lawson, or I'm going to be in
BIG trouble when I get home.
Let's wait a few minutes
until they start singing and
then we can play tic-tac-toe or
hangman or something.

V

River Road
Belington, WV 26250
September 1, 1996

Abigail Van Buren
P.O. Box 447
Mount Morris, IL 61054–0447

Dear Abby,

Please help me, for I am having problems with my best girlfriend of almost twelve years. I will not give her name because, first, I am not saying it ever again and, second, because she would kill me if it came out in the paper. Let's just call her Touchy.

Okay, here's what happened, and you tell me who's right.

Sal—, I mean, Touchy and I were playing games in church because we got tired of giving people fashion violations for ugly clothes. So we started playing tic-tac-toe and hangman. Touchy always beats me at tic-tac-toe, but I'm pretty good at hangman because I can think of words that

124

don't have any vowels or T's, R's, S's, L's, or N's in them.

Touchy wanted to use exotic flowers for some reason I can't say, and I wanted to do TV shows, but we compromised and guessed rock stars. She never has gotten the hang of the game and always gives me her favorites. All I have to do is count the blanks and guess "Madonna" or "Whitney Houston."

I always stump her, even if I use the same one over and over. She should have learned over the years not to use any of the common guesses. But let me tell you about today.

"E," she started.

"No. That's one," I said as I drew the little head hanging down from the noose.

"A?"

"Nope," and on went the straight line for his body.

"O? There's got to be an 'o'!"

"Uh-uh." Left arm.

"U????"

"Guess again." Right arm.

"Did I say 'i' yet?"

"No 'i', and you have one more chance," I said as I drew on the left leg.

"One more? Give me shoes, too. You gave me shoes the last time."

Sometimes I draw on extra parts for her hangman when I want to prolong her suffering, but I was getting bored, plus Reverend Lawson was winding down.

"Nope. One try," I said.

"Fine! 'R' then. There has to be a 'r'!"

She had forgot who she was dealing with, and I drew on the right leg and let her stickman blow in the wind.

"You're dead," I said, and closed up the little spiral notebook I carry in my purse for just such occasions.

"Well what is it then if there isn't any a, e, i, o, or u? There's got to be a vowel. Is there a 'y'?"

"Nope."

"Tell me."

"Guess."

"No, I quit."

"Oh okay. Have you never heard of the 'B-52s'?"

"You have to use the 'the' in that case."

"No way. And it wouldn't have helped you anyway. You'd have had one measly 'e'."

"I can't believe you would cheat me in a church. You're sicker than I thought!"

"Cheat? You didn't use the 'the' in 'Rolling Stones'!"

"Well that's different. They are well known."

"Yeah, right."

126

"You're not supposed to use numbers. You're supposed to spell out numbers."

"I've never seen anyone spell out numbers in my life. You never can face it when you've been outsmarted."

"Forget it then. I'll never play any of your dumb games again."

"Fine."

"Double fine!"

So here's my question, Dear Abby, are you supposed to spell out numbers or not?

Sincerly,

V. M. Cutright

P.S. Just because someone is old doesn't make that person boring and unimportant, does it?

River Road
Belington, WV 26250
September 4, 1996

Mr. John Casto
Circulation Director
The Elkins Exponent
Elkins, WV 26241

Dear Mr. Casto:

I hope you won't get mad, but I have something awful to tell you. I won't be able to deliver all my papers once school starts back. Daddy and Mama say that once the time changes it will be dark before I could get them all delivered. Plus, I have to allow some time for homework. YUCK!

Do you know someone who could take over half of the route? I asked my friend Sally if she would split it with me, but she just wrinkled her nose and said she wasn't sure girls should be seen out peddling papers and yakking with old folks. CAN YOU BELIEVE THAT?!? Who wouldn't want the chance to make their own money? Plus, it was just a nasty thing for her to say, being that she knows that I am a girl AND I deliver papers. And what business is it of HERS who I spend my time with!!! Sometimes I wonder if she and I are really best friends. All she thinks about is clothes and boys—which are both okay—but there's more to life than just those two things, don't you think?

P.S. If you can't find someone to take part of my route right away, I won't leave you in a bind, so don't worry—but please hurry!

P.P.S. Thank you for the opportunity to work for you. Because of my route I will be able to have a lot of new school clothes. Not as many as Prissy Missy, but plenty for me—especially since I mostly like jeans and T-shirts!

Sincerely,

Venola Mae

River Road
Belington, WV 26250
September 9, 1996

Mr. John Casto
Circulation Director
<u>The Elkins Exponent</u>
Elkins, WV 26241

Dear Mr. Casto:

Would you really miss my letters?!? You are a very nice boss. The best one I've ever had. (Ha! Ha!) Don't worry—I'm not quitting entirely, and I'll still keep you posted on things even after school starts.

P.S. You can always write or call me if the person who takes over the other half of my route gets sick or freaks out or anything.

P.P.S. Am I <u>REALLY</u> the best paper carrier you've ever had? Even better than my brothers?!?

Sincerely,

Venola Mae

  2 newspaper people
+2 keep in touch
  ─────────────────
  4 ever!

River Road
Belington, WV 26250
Friday the 13th! 1996

Abigail Van Buren
P.O. Box 447
Mount Morris, IL 61054–0447

Dear Abby,

Your advice stinks. What do you mean me and
Touchy shouldn't have been playing games in
church at all and from now on we should pay
attention to the preacher? You don't EVEN know
how boring Reverend Lawson is!

And anyway, we kind of made up on our own
without any advice from you. So maybe I'll just
write to your bosses and tell them how mean you
can be.

P.S. I didn't write to you for a spelling lesson.
Who cares if you can spell <u>sincerely</u> and I can't? I
am only in seventh grade. I am in "I" spelling
book, which is the most advanced. I <u>can</u> spell
<u>sincerely</u>, but I was in a hurry to get your advice.

P.P.S. What about that age question I asked you at the end. Did you forget to read the P.S.?

Sincerely,

V. M. Cutright
Paper Carrier of the Summer

River Road
Belington, WV 26250
September 24, 1996

Bosses of Abigail Van Buren
P.O. Box 447
Mount Morris, IL 61054–0447

Dear Dear Abby's Bosses:

Your employee isn't that smart. She gives advice about as good as a sea monkey! See attached letters for more details.

I think you should call Miss Wilma Facemeir at (304) 555–1234 and give her Dear Abby's job. She is lots smarter and not snobby at all.

Thank you for your time.

Sincerely,

Venola Mae Cutright

P.S. I am also in the newspaper business.

River Road
Belington, WV 26250
September 27, 1996

Imperial Magic Sea Monkey Company
P.O. Box 2000
Destin, FL 32541

Dear Brine Shrimp People:

Thank you for the FULL refund (plus shipping and handling!) and the advice to find a pen pal in journalism or politics. Do you think Diane Sawyer would write to me? What about Hillary or Chelsea Clinton? I have a few ideas for them. I had been thinking about contacting that poor LaToya Jackson at the Psychic Network. She has a lot of troublesome brothers too and could probably use a friend. But then maybe I should mind my own business and stay out of someone else's family problems. I wouldn't want anyone butting into one of Bobby and my arguments! Anyway, if LaToya's really a psychic, she would know what I was going to write before I wrote it, and that might get on my nerves and be a waste of time. It is nice of your company to take such a personal interest in the lives of your customers.

P.S. Yes, I did already send your name into "Consumer Crackdown." Sorry.

P.P.S. I promise to let you know ALL ABOUT my new pen pal the minute I hear anything.

Your forever friend,

Venola Mae Cutright
Future Marine Biologist
(or barefoot water-skier)